W9-CJE-452

Purchased with a grant from
Carl & Verna Schmidt
Foundation

BEING FRANK

Written by Donna W. Earnhardt

Illustrated by Andrea Castellani

Flash
Light PRESS

Printed in China. First Edition — October 2012   Library of Congress Control Number: 2012932503

ISBN 978-1-9362611-9-2

Editor: Shari Dash Greenspan   Graphic Design: The Virtual Paintbrush

This book was typeset in Henhouse. The illustrations were rendered in Photoshop.

Distributed by IPG.

Flashlight Press, 527 Empire Blvd., Brooklyn, NY 11225
www.FlashlightPress.com

To my sweet family of "Franks,"
I love you all. —DE

To Ilaria and Damiano,
thanks for the patience. —AC

Frank was always frank.

"Honesty is the best policy," he said.

Frank never lied to his schoolmates.

"Your freckles remind me of the Big Dipper," he told Dotty.
Dotty pulled her hood over her face.

"Your singing is kind of shrieky," Frank told Carol.
Carol stomped away.

Frank always told the truth to adults.

"Your breath smells funny," he told his teacher, Ms. Zaroma.

She sent Frank to the principal's office.

"Your toupée looks like my pet weasel," he told Principal Wiggins.

Mr. Wiggins called Frank's mom.

"You wouldn't get so many wrinkles if you didn't glare at me like that," Frank told his mom on the way home. "And by the way — you're speeding."

And Frank was always,
ALWAYS honest with
police officers.

"Yes, officer," he said. "She knew
how fast she was going. I told her."

Frank was very proud of being frank.

But other than police officers, adults weren't as impressed with Frank's honesty as he thought they should be.

"You'll have wrinkles one day, too," Mom said, rubbing on some lotion.

"Some things are better left unsaid," said Mr. Wiggins, adjusting his toupée.

"You don't have to say everything you're thinking." said Ms. Zaroma, popping a mint in her mouth.

Frank's schoolmates weren't impressed either.

"My freckles do NOT look lik[e] the Big Dipper," Dotty said. "And my mother says I shouldn't listen to you."

"I'm still going to sing in the talent show at the school carnival tomorrow — but I'm not going to ride the Ferris wheel with you," Carol told Frank.

"But we always ride the Ferris wheel together," Frank whispered.

Everyone was upset, and now Frank wasn't so happy either.

Frank clipped his toenails and alphabetized his bug collection, but he didn't feel any better, so he walked down the block to Grandpa's house.

Grandpa Ernest was on the porch clipping his toenails. "Incoming!" he yelled.

Frank ducked.

"What's up, Frank?" Grandpa said.

"Everyone is mad at me for being frank. I'm not sure honesty is the best policy anymore."

"That used to happen to me, too," said Grandpa.

Mrs. Peacock walked by and straightened her massive hat. "It's new! Do you like it, Ernest?"

Frank thought the hat looked like a flower store on Mrs. Peacock's head.

"Well," Grandpa said, "there are an awful lot of flowers up there. But my favorite is the purple one in the middle."

"Thank you!" Mrs. Peacock beamed. "Toodle-oo!"

Frank couldn't believe his ears. "Grandpa, you lied!"

"No, Frank, I told the truth. I really do like the purple flower best. I talked about the good things on her hat instead of the not-so-good things."

Grandpa's best friend, Mr. Pickles, pulled up in his truck. "Try this relish," he called, handing Grandpa a jar and a spoon. "I've got a cold and can't taste a thing."

Grandpa scooped a spoonful of relish into his mouth.
His nose twitched.   His eyes watered.   His hair stood on end.

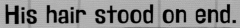

"Give it to me straight, Ernest," said Mr. Pickles.
"I can't sell it if it's no good."

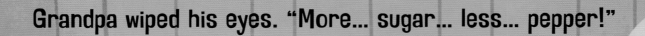

Grandpa wiped his eyes. "More... sugar... less... pepper!"

Mr. Pickles grinned and shook Grandpa's hand. "Back to the drawing board! Thanks for your help!"

"Grandpa, he didn't get mad at you!"

"That's right." Grandpa drank some water. "He asked me for the truth — and I gave it to him."

Frank sighed. "So I shouldn't give the truth unless someone asks for it?"

"You should always give people the truth," Grandpa said. "You just have to find the right way to serve it."

The next afternoon at the school carnival, when Ms. Zaroma laughed like a horse, Frank said, "You tell great jokes." When Mr. Wiggins did a weird dance, Frank said, "Impressive spins, sir!"

When Frank saw Dotty, he said, "I like dots better than squares." And when Carol sang, Frank said, "You sure can hit those high notes."

Carol smiled at Frank. "Dotty and I are going to ride the Ferris wheel. Want to come?"

On the way home, Frank gave his mom a poem he wrote for her.

And when she smiled, Frank decided not to mention the wrinkles around the corners of her mouth.

The next day, while Frank helped Grandpa in his garden, Mrs. Peacock stopped by again. "You were right!" she said to Grandpa. "That other hat had too many flowers."

Just then, Mr. Pickles arrived with a new jar of relish for Grandpa to try.

"Excuse me a moment," Grandpa said to Mrs. Peacock.

"So, what do you think of my hat?"
Mrs. Peacock asked.

But this time, she wasn't asking Grandpa.
She was asking Frank.

Frank looked at Grandpa on the porch with Mr. Pickles. Grandpa was taking another spoonful of relish, and he wasn't drinking any water.

Frank knew just what to say. "I've never seen a hat like that before. It must be one of a kind."

"Thank you!" Mrs. Peacock beamed. "Toodle-oo!"

"So how is it being Frank today?" Grandpa asked.

"Well, Grandpa, I still think honesty is the best policy," said Frank, "but now I know it's best served with more sugar..."